To
SKYLAR,

From

....

You may have heard the stories?
I tell you they are true!
A superhero lives nearby.
But where? I wish I knew!

WHO IS OUR HERO?

She's got an "S" upon her suit,
Her cape is long and flowing.

Who is the girl behind the mask?
There's just no way of knowing!

They say she's very clever.
She's brave and fast and strong.
Do you know who she is yet?
Her name's SIX letters long!

Oh no! A cat's stuck up a tree!
But who will get it out?
Our hero stops and says,
"I'll use my. . .

SUPER SKYLAR SHOUT!!!"

This little girl is crying.
Her trike has got a flat.

I guess it must be hungry work
When one is fighting crime.
She runs and jumps and dives around.
She's moving all the time!

Super Skylar is so strong,
She simply can't be beaten.
It must be all the salad, sprouts,
And broccoli she's eaten!

There's trouble on the playground!
Kids start to scream and shout.

Super Skylar, kind and true,
Knows how to work this out!

Uh-oh! That child's about to fall.
He'll get a nasty scrape!

But never fear,
For guess who's here?
Our hero in a cape!

She's the world's best superhero.
And she's got a super cuddle!

The next time you're in trouble,
Or ever in harm's way, shout. . .

This superhero stuff's hard work,
And now she's very sleepy,
But Super Skylar feels afraid–
Her bedroom looks so creepy!

Yet heroes do not run or hide
When they are feeling scared!
Instead they face their fears head on.
That's why she's come prepared!

She's caring and she's helpful,
Always doing awesome deeds.
Yes, Super Skylar is the hero
Everybody needs!

She's always super-wonderful.
She's super-terrific, too.
Just who is Super Skylar?
WAIT! I think it must be...

Written by Eric James
Illustrated by Steve Brown
Designed by Ryan Dunn

Copyright © Hometown World Ltd 2018

Put Me In The Story is a
registered trademark of Sourcebooks, Inc.
All rights reserved.

Published by Put Me In The Story,
a publication of Sourcebooks, Inc.
P.O. Box 4410, Naperville, Illinois 60567-4410
(630) 961-3900
www.putmeinthestory.com

Date of Production: October 2018
Run Number: HTW_PO201833
Printed and bound in Italy (LG)
10 9 8 7 6 5 4 3 2 1

Bestselling books starring your child!
www.putmeinthestory.com

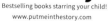